Hide and Seek

A las escondidas

by Deborah Schecter

ISBN: 978-1-338-70288-0
Illustrated by Anne Kennedy

Published by Scholastic Inc., 557 Broadway, New York, NY 10012

10 9 8 7 6 68 23 24 25 26/0

Printed in Jiaxing, China. First printing, June 2020.

SCHOLASTIC

Where can I hide?

¿Dónde me puedo esconder?

I can hide behind a chair.

Me puedo esconder detrás
de un sillón.

I can hide behind my hair.

Me puedo esconder detrás de mi pelo.

I can hide in a dress.

Me puedo esconder dentro de un vestido.

I can hide in a mess.

Me puedo esconder en
el desorden.

I can hide under the rug.

Me puedo esconder debajo
de la alfombra.

I can hide in a hug!

¡Me puedo esconder
en un abrazo!